Big Chris's Big Workout

First published in Great Britain by HarperCollins Children's Books in 2007

10 9 8 7 6 5 4 3

ISBN-10: 0-00-725306-0   ISBN-13: 978-0-00-725306-7

© Chapman Entertainment Limited & David Jenkins 2007

A CIP catalogue record for this title is available from the British Library.

Based on the television series Roary the Racing Car and the original script
'Big Chris's Big Workout' by Wayne Jackman.
© Chapman Entertainment Limited & David Jenkins 2007

Visit Roary at: www.roarytheracingcar.com

Printed and bound in Italy by LEGO

Big Chris's Big Workout

HarperCollins Children's Books

It was early morning at Silver Hatch. In the workshop, Roary and his friends were all fast asleep. Well, almost all of them...

"Rise and shine, Roary!" whispered Cici. "Coming for a spin or is Roary a little sleepyhead?" she teased as she rolled quietly out of the workshop.

"Me!" asked Roary, stifling a yawn. "We'll see who's a sleepyhead. Race you!"

And with that, the pair zoomed off round Silver Hatch race track.

Across the track, Big Chris was getting up too. He was looking for his most favourite thing in the entire world – his doughnut.

"There you are, my beauty," he said, holding up the doughnut and licking his lips. "But there's no room for you in my lunchbox!"

Big Chris looked down at his already full sandwich box. "Sorry sarnies," he said, throwing them out of the box and replacing them with the doughnut. "Oh, I can't wait till lunchtime."

Cici and Roary were far too busy racing around Silver Hatch to worry about lunch!

They zoomed down the straights, squealed around corners and leapt over Tummy Turn Bridge.

"Catch me if you can, Roary!" called Cici.

"I will," said Roary "Just you wait and see!"

Just as Cici thought she had the race sewn up, Roary inched ahead of her.

But he was going too fast to see Hare-Pin Bend ahead. "Woooaaahhh!" Roary yelled as he spun off the track. He crashed through the tyre wall and into a big muddy puddle.

"Eurgh!" said a very muddy, very unhappy Flash, who had been watching the race.

"Roary!" called Cici. "Are you alright?" Roary tried to drive out of the mud but his wheels just whizzed around and around. "No, I'm stuck," he moaned.

"Don't worry," yelled Cici as she sped off. "I'll go and get Big Chris!"

"Spanner," said Big Chris. He was hard at work and Molecom was doing his best to help. He squinted into Big Chris's lunchbox but instead of a spanner, he passed Chris his doughnut!

"That's not a spanner!" Big Chris sighed. But the doughnut did look good. "Oh, it's the crunchy hundreds and thousands that do it for me. I think I'll just have one bite…"

"Big Chris!" called Cici. "Roary is stuck in the mud at Hare-Pin Bend!"

Roary was just starting to wonder if anyone was coming for him when Marsha appeared on Zippee. "Oh my goodness," she said, spotting the muddy little car. "How did you end up here, Roary?"

"I took the bend too quickly, Marsha," Roary confessed. "And now I'm stuck!"

"It's alright, Roary, Big Chris is on his way!" came a voice over the hill. It was Cici! "Come on Zippee, if we work together we can pull him out."

Roary grabbed on to his friends and slowly but surely, they pulled him out of the mud.

Just as Roary pulled back onto the track, Big Chris appeared. He puffed and panted all the way down.

"Don't worry," he gasped. "I'm here –"

"I think someone needs a bit more exercise," Marsha smiled.

"I get as much exercise..." Big Chris bent over and tried to catch his breath, "...as you do, Marsha."

"I go for a run every morning," Marsha said. "Do you?"

"Well, maybe not every morning," Big Chris panted. "But I bet I'm fitter than you are."

"Why don't we find out?" Marsha grinned, stretching. "We'll each run around the track and whoever has the fastest time wins. Unless you don't feel up to it…"

"Eh, who's not up to it? You're on!" Big Chris said.

Back at the starting line, Marsha was well into her warm up.

She stretched happily, looking forward to her run.

Molecom took the stopwatch and the chequered flag as

Marsha got into position. All the cars were there – it would

be fun to watch someone else race for a change!

As she took pole position, the lights lit up above Marsha.

One red light.

Two red lights

Three red lights.

Four and five red lights.

When all five lights went out, Marsha took off round the track. Up the hills and round the bends and in no time at all, she was at the finishing line.

"Wahay, Marsha!" cried Molecom. "Ten minutes and twenty seconds!"

"Your turn now, Big Chris," Marsha smiled.

"Can't wait," he gave her his biggest, broadest smile.

"As soon as I've had my lunch." But when Big Chris opened his lunchbox, it was empty! He looked up and spotted Flash hopping onto his skateboard with his delicious doughnut.

"My doughnut!" he shouted, suddenly sprinting after Flash. "Come back here you rabbit rascal!"

"Is this what you're looking for, Big Chris?" Flash waved the doughnut from the back of his skateboard. But Big Chris was not about to give in and lose his precious pastry. He chased Flash all around the track, not even pausing for breath. Soon, they were almost back at the finish line, where Flash had a spectacular crash! Everyone was cheering Big Chris on and without even realising, Big Chris had completed the race!

"That's mine, you rotten rabbit!" Big Chris shouted at Flash. He tried to grab the doughnut as it flew out of Flash's hand, and slipped to the ground.

"Ten minutes and fifteen seconds!" announced Molecom. "Big Chris is the winner!"

"Congratulations, Big Chris!" grinned Marsha.

"Yay," cheered Roary. "Nice one, Big Chris."

"Thanks, Roary," sighed Big Chris, eyeing his ruined doughnut.
"But look at this! It's so dirty, I'll have to throw it away."
"Have one of my sandwiches instead," said Marsha as she
offered Big Chris a healthy lettuce and tomato sandwich.
He took it, looked at it, sniffed it and then took a little bite.
"Eh, that's tasty, that is!" he grinned, munching away.
And so, after a hard morning's exercise, Big Chris filled up his
tank with a healthier type of fuel.

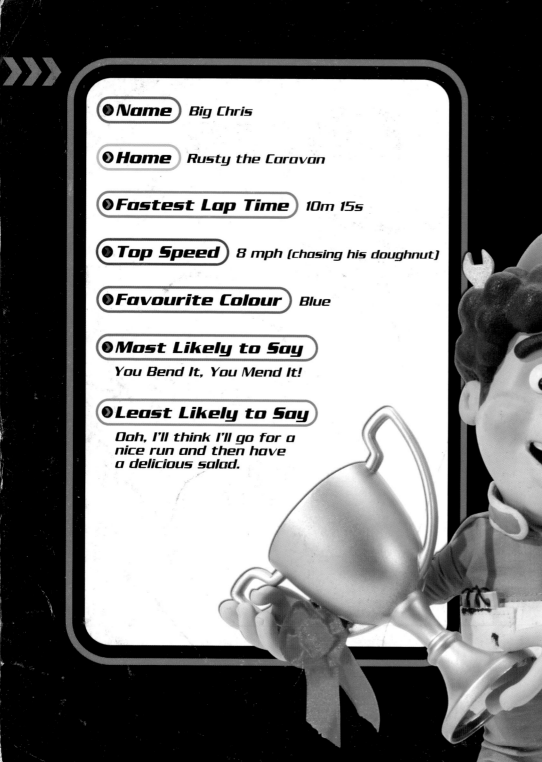

Name Big Chris

Home Rusty the Caravan

Fastest Lap Time 10m 15s

Top Speed 8 mph (chasing his doughnut)

Favourite Colour Blue

Most Likely to Say

You Bend It, You Mend It!

Least Likely to Say

Ooh, I'll think I'll go for a
nice run and then have
a delicious salad.

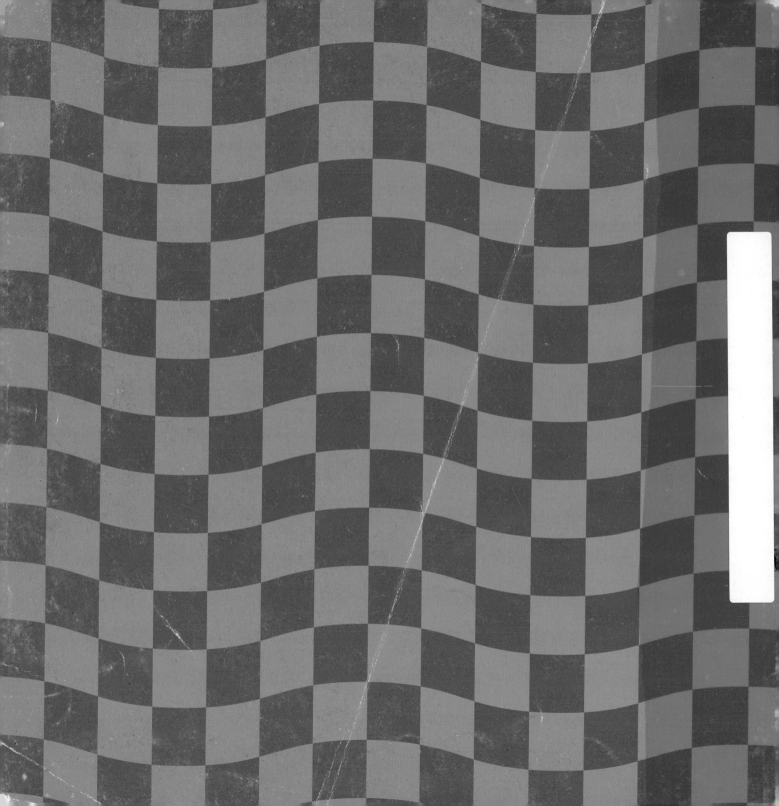